JOURNEY TO THE WEST SERIES 2

Monkey King Creates Havoc in Heaven

GUANBIN CARTOON STUDIO

Australia Multiculture Press

Monkey King Creates Havoc in Heaven

"Journey to the West" Series Book ②

ISBN: 1-921099-01-1
First edition 2005
First printing 2005

Publisher: Australia Multiculture Press
        Suite 23,301 Castlereagh Street
        Sydney N S W 2000, Australia
Illustration: Guanbin Studio
Printed in P. R. China

Price: A$ 12.00   US$ 10.00

The Monkey King had studied how to become immortal under Patriarch Subhuti so now, after much practice, he was very skilled at magic.

On his return home to Hua Guo Mountain he trained the monkeys in how to use weapons.

One day during practice, he leapt down amongst the monkeys to show them a few tricks with his large, gleaming sword.

The monkeys were applauding the Monkey King's performance when, without warning, his sword snapped in two. He was very annoyed.

An old monkey came forward to tell him that he could get a very fine weapon from the Dragon King of the Eastern Ocean.

The Monkey King was so pleased to hear this that he leapt straight into the sea and headed for the palace of the Dragon King.

When the Dragon King came out to meet him, the Monkey King told him that he wanted a fine weapon.

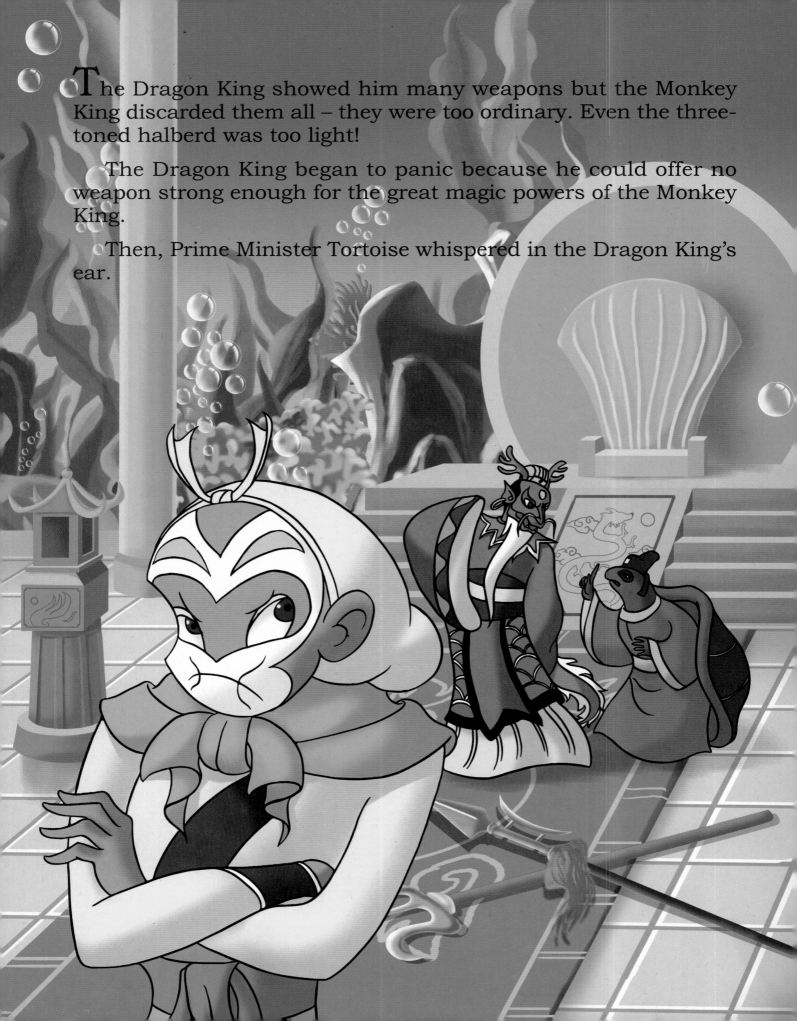

The Dragon King showed him many weapons but the Monkey King discarded them all – they were too ordinary. Even the three-toned halberd was too light!

The Dragon King began to panic because he could offer no weapon strong enough for the great magic powers of the Monkey King.

Then, Prime Minister Tortoise whispered in the Dragon King's ear.

The Dragon King escorted the Monkey King to the bottom of the sea where something golden was shining.

"This is one of the magic pins the Dayu used to fix the sea in place when he controlled the floods. If you can shift it, it's yours".

The Monkey King rushed at it.

The magic pin was a one-hundred-foot long pillar of iron, so thick that the Monkey King could barely get his arms around it.

"I wish it was smaller," he muttered.

Instantly, the pillar shrank and the Monkey King heaved it out, rocking the entire Dragon Palace.

"Shrink!" commanded the Monkey King and the gleaming, gold-banded cudgel shrank further to the size of an embroidery needle that he tucked behind his ear.

"Thanks," he called as he rushed off before the Dragon King could change his mind.

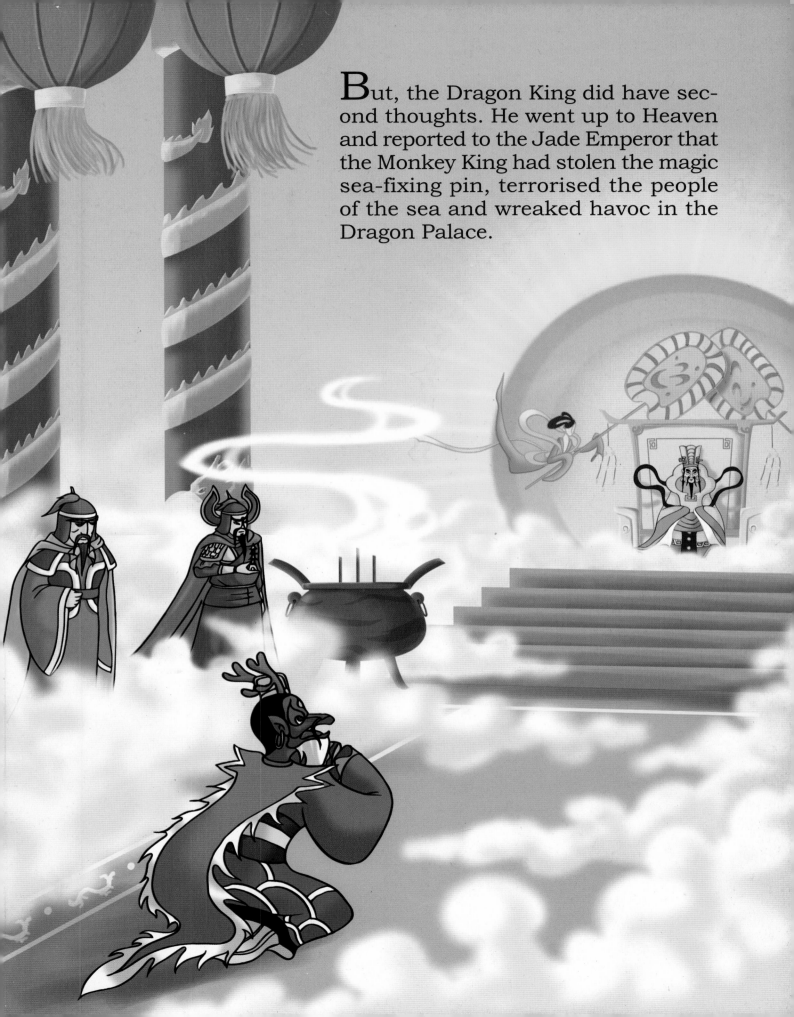

But, the Dragon King did have second thoughts. He went up to Heaven and reported to the Jade Emperor that the Monkey King had stolen the magic sea-fixing pin, terrorised the people of the sea and wreaked havoc in the Dragon Palace.

The Jade Emperor wanted to know more about this Monkey King.

Tai Bai Xing explained that the Monkey King was immortal, that he had great magic powers and that he should not be underestimated.

He then suggested that maybe the Monkey King should be invited to Heaven so that they could keep him under control.

The Jade Emperor agreed this was a good plan.

Back on Hua Guo Mountain, the Monkey King was showing off his new treasure to the monkeys when Tai Bai Xing arrived to issue the Jade Emperor's invitation for the Monkey King to go to Heaven.

"What fun!" thought the Monkey King. "Keep up your weapons training while I am away," he called to the monkeys.

With one somersault, the Monkey King sped off, leaving Tai Bai Xing struggling to catch up.

When the guards at the Southern Gate of Heaven refused to let him in, the Monkey King lost his temper and was just about to attack with his magic cudgel when Tai Bai Xing arrived and gave the authority for the Monkey King to enter Heaven.

The Monkey King strode straight into the Hall of Miraculous Mist without bowing to the Jade Emperor.

Tai Bai Xing tried to excuse the Monkey King's disrespect by explaining, "This wicked immortal from the lower world has no manners."

Unperturbed, the Jade Emperor announced, "I appoint you Protector of Horses." "Bow to the ground and thank his Majesty," Tai Bai Xing prompted, but the Monkey King ignored him.

After the Monkey King had left, the Jade Emperor ordered the Keeper of the Imperial Stud to keep the monkey under tight control.

The Keeper understood the message.

In the Heavenly Stables, the Monkey King found that the horses, tethered to posts, were listless and in poor spirits.

He immediately set them free to gallop around the grounds.

As well, he turned clouds into rain to give them a shower and he fed and cared for them so well that they all gained weight.

One day the Keeper of the Imperial Stud arrived unannounced. When he found the horses running loose he demanded to know who had let them out.

Then he scolded the Monkey King for not taking proper care of the horses. "My task is to keep you under control," he shouted angrily.

The Monkey King was furious at the Emperor's trick so he tore off his uniform, threw it down and flew off.

The Monkey King smashed the stables with his gold-banded cudgel, fought his way through the Southern Gate and returned to Hua Guo Mountain.

When the Jade Emperor heard all this, he was very upset. He ordered Heavenly King Li, the Grand Demon-subduing Marshal, to lead his armies down to earth to capture the Monkey King.

When Heavenly King Li, with his son, Nezha, and the Mighty Spirit arrived at Hua Guo Mountain with their armies, they found the Monkey King's banner flying high.

GREAT SAGE EQUAL-LING HEAVEN, it proclaimed.

The Mighty Spirit charged forward to tackle the Monkey King but was hit so hard by the cudgel that he collapsed. Although he stormed and raged, the Might Spirit could not get close to the Monkey King.

Then, on the Monkey King's command, the cudgel grew so big that the Mighty Spirit was pinned helplessly to the ground while little monkeys ran all over him, pinching and scratching.

Next, baby-faced Nezha took up the battle against the Monkey King.

Nezha called on magic to give him three heads and six arms but the Monkey King also used magic to turn three hairs into three monkeys who carried on the fight with Nezha while the Monkey King sat and watched from a nearby cloud.

Recognising the trick, Nezha threw out his Wind-fire Rings which burned up the three imitation monkeys.

The Monkey King turned himself into a Wind-fire Ring and hurled himself towards Nezha.

Thinking it was one of his own Rings, Nezha stepped on it, burnt himself and then fell over on the cloud. He limped away beaten.

Things were going so badly that Heavenly King Li decided to withdraw his troops.

He turned them into a black cloud and flew back to the Heavenly Palace.

The Monkey King and his monkey helpers laughed and cheered as they celebrated their victory.

Back in the Heavenly Palace, the Jade Emperor was enjoying delightful music when Heavenly King Li rushed in and reported that they had lost the battle.

The news shocked the Jade Emperor. He sat deep in thought while Tai Bai Xing and Heavenly King Li discussed their next move.

Heavenly King Li insisted they should send more soldiers but Tai Bai Xing disagreed. He thought they should allow the Monkey King to keep his title but lure him back to Heaven where he could be kept under control.

The Jade Emperor agreed with Tai Bai Xing's plan. "We could put him in charge of the Queen Mother's Peach Garden."

Later, on Hua Guo Mountain, a crowd of monkeys dragged the struggling Tai Bai Xing to their honourable king and declared, "Your majesty. We have caught a spy!"

Tai Bai Xing struggled to his feet, tidied himself and began to flatter the Monkey King.

"Please come back to heaven. The Jade Emperor has appointed you Great Sage Equalling Heaven."

The Monkey King brushed off the offer. "I already have that title here on Hua Guo Mountain," he replied. "I don't need the Jade Emperor to give me the title."

Tai Bai Xing quickly tried another ploy.

"How about being in charge of the Queen Mother's Peach Garden? The Garden is even more beautiful than this mountain."

The Monkey King fell for the trick and accepted the offer. He received his title from the Jade Emperor and then, dressed in the robes of a Great Sage, somersaulted off to the Peach Garden.

The Garden God met the Monkey King at the gate of the Peach Garden and escorted him on a tour of inspection.

The Monkey King, impressed by the enormous magic peaches, was just about to pick one when the Garden God stopped him.

"You can't do that!" he cried. "The peaches can only be eaten at the Queen Mother's Peach Banquet."

The Monkey King suggested that the Garden God should take a break.

As soon as the Garden God was out of sight, the Monkey King jumped into the tree and ate some of the biggest magic peaches.

Feeling very contented, he shrank himself to a few inches, covered himself with a peach leaf and fell asleep on a branch.

Some time later the Queen Mother sent seven fairy maidens to pick peaches for the Peach Banquet. As they picked the peaches, the fairy maidens noticed something wrong.

"Why are so many peaches missing?" they wondered.

One of the fairy maidens, seeing some big peaches on a high branch, pulled the branch down.

It was the branch where the Monkey King was sleeping!

The movement woke the Monkey King and returned him to his original size.

The sight of him terrified the fairy maidens so they flew back to a safe distance while they told him about the Peach Banquet.

They listed all the honoured guests but the Monkey King was not one of them. Furious that he had been tricked again, the Monkey King hurled curses at the Jade Emperor and immobilised the fairy maidens with a magic spell.

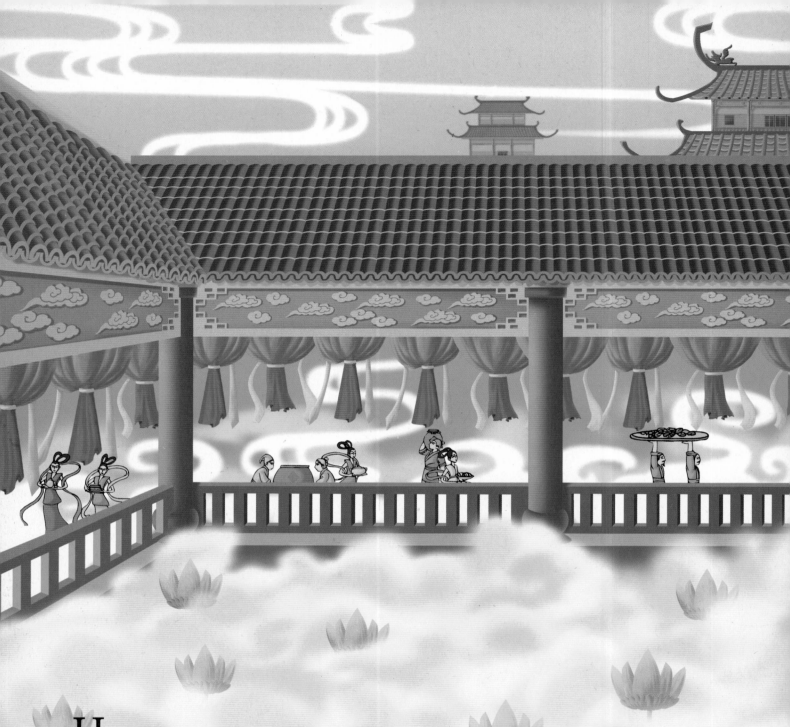

He flew to the Queen Mother's Jade Pool where beautiful clouds glowed with colour above the pool's crystal waters and a dazzling pearl danced in the waters of a fountain surrounded by carved jade rocks.

Nearby, coloured lanterns and incense decorated the Jade Pool Pavilion.

Servants carrying huge jars of magic wine were preparing for the Banquet.

The Monkey King pulled out some of his hairs, blew on them and turned them into hundreds of sleep insects which bit the immortal officials and servants, promptly sending them to sleep.

The Monkey King sat down at the banquet table, poured himself a cup of wine and gloated, "You didn't invite me to the Peach Banquet, but here I am!"

He proceeded to drink the wine and gobble the food.

Remembering his fellow monkeys back home, the Monkey King called forth a magic sack into which he loaded all the marvellous banquet food.

He tied the sack around his waist and staggered off on his cloud.

Too tipsy to return to Hua Guo Mountain, the Monkey King flew to the Tushita Palace of the Supreme Lord Lao Zi in the Thirty Third Heaven instead.

The Monkey King charged into Tushita Palace and shouted but the main hall was dark and deserted.

He explored further and found the Elixir Pill Room with a large bronze bell glowing a peculiar colour.

Under the bell was a gourd full of Golden Elixir Pills that the Monkey King scooped up and swallowed. As his body began to glow, he realised that he could be in terrible trouble and, with one somersault, headed to Hua Guo Mountain.

Back at the Shui Lian Cave, the Monkey King shared the magic food at a banquet.

As the magic peaches, wine and food came flying out of the sack, the monkeys cheered and celebrated the return of their King.

Meanwhile, the Queen Mother, shocked to find the banquet at the Jade Pool Pavilion wrecked, went to complain to the Jade Emperor.

At the same time, the Supreme Lord Lao Zi was complaining to the Jade Emperor that the Monkey King had eaten all the Elixir Pills.

The Jade Emperor was so furious that he ordered Heavenly King Li and a hundred thousand soldiers to capture the wicked Monkey King.

As the armies drew up ready for battle, the Monkey King stood proudly at the head of his army, his *Great Sage Equalling Heaven* banner billowing in the breeze.

The Sword Heaven King threw his sword at the Monkey King and it turned into thousand of little swords. The Monkey King calmly turned some hairs into thousands of little shields and the swords shattered.

Next, the Lute Heaven King started to play his magic lute. The sound made the monkey soldiers and their leader feel weak.

Then the Umbrella Heaven King brought out his magic umbrella. It created a dark mist that sucked the monkeys into the umbrella.

The two Kings laughed triumphantly as they put away the lute and umbrella.

The Monkey King poked at the umbrella with his cudgel but it made no impression.

Then, he turned one of his hairs into a steel gimlet which, with a few thrusts, made a hole large enough for all the monkeys to escape.

The Monkey King seized the lute and, with one great pull, broke all the strings with an ear-splitting twang.

The two Kings fled!

Finally, the Snake Heaven King released his deadly snake with its long red tongue.

As the Monkey King struggled with the deadly snake he noticed a pearl on its head. He grabbed the pearl and the snake died.

Seeing the four Heavenly Kings beaten made the God Erlang roar in anger and charge at the Monkey King with his Heaven Hound. A fierce struggle ensued. Meantime, the Heavenly Armies tried to storm Shui Lian Cave.

The monkeys turned the waterfall on the soldiers like a hose and then entangled them in creepers. But, the next attack came with fire and arrows and the monkeys had to pull back.

W hen the Monkey King saw what was happening he tried to escape from Erlang.

He changed into a sparrow, but Erlang became an eagle. He changed into a fish, but Erlang became an egret.

So, he became a local temple. Erling shot a beam of magic light out of the third eye in his forehead and saw that the temple was really the Monkey King.

The struggle continued. Supreme Lord Lao Zi, who was watching from the clouds, realised that Erling could not win so he took a special bracelet from his arm and threw it at the Monkey King from behind. It hit the Monkey King on the head and he collapsed.

The Heaven Hound pounced on him and the Monkey King was captured.

The Jade Emperor considered every horrible way to kill the Monkey King. It was a challenge because the Monkey King could not be cut by blades nor burned by fire.

Finally, the Emperor gave him to the Supreme Lord Lao Zi to cook in the furnace used for making immortality pills.

After forty-nine days there was no sound from the furnace.

"Open the furnace!" ordered Lord Lao Zi.

The fiery golden lights that could be seen when the door opened were not immortality pills, as Lord Lao Zi thought, but were the Monkey King's eyes.

The Monkey King leapt from the furnace, bit Lord Lao Zi hard, kicked over the furnace and sped off to the Hall of the Miraculous Mist in a streak of golden light.

The Monkey King fought his way into the Jade Emperor's Palace, scattering Heavenly Generals in his wake as he headed to the Hall of Miraculous Mist.

Once there, the Monkey King smashed the stone columns and the palace collapsed in ruins.

The Monkey King laughed jubilantly at his amazing triumph.